WARNING!

THESE JOKES WILL ANNOY EVERY DAD

WARNING!

THESE JOKES WILL ANNOY EVERY DAD

PENGUIN BOOKS

What's the difference between a bad joke and a dad joke?

The letter D.

Why don't skeletons fight each other?

They don't have the guts.

Why does a chicken coop only have two doors?

Because if it had four, it would be a sedan.

What is the easiest building to lift?

A lighthouse.

Why do cardigans hang out together?

They're very close-knit.

Why did the zombie take a nap?

It was dead tired.

Why are frogs good at baseball?

They know how to catch fly balls.

Did you hear about the archeologist who got fired?

His career is in ruins.

Why shouldn't you tell secrets in a cornfield?

There are too many ears around.

What happens when two rowboats get into an argument?

It can be an oar-deal.

Did you hear about the cleaners who went to space?

They ended up scrubbing the mission.

What did the beach say when the tide came in?

'Long time, no sea.'

Why are turkeys such good percussionists?

They have drumsticks.

What two things should you never eat for breakfast?

Lunch and dinner.

How do you make a robot angry?

Keep pushing its buttons.

Why did the orchestra get struck by lightning?

It had a conductor.

How much does it cost to swim with sharks?

An arm and a leg.

I have never been a fan of facial hair . . .
But now it's starting to grow on me.

I'm so good at sleeping . . .
I can do it with my eyes closed.

What did one toilet say to the other?

'You look flushed.'

Why are so many people tired on 1 April?

They have just finished a 31-day March.

How do you make a tissue dance?

Put a little boogie in it.

Our vacuum cleaner is getting old . . .

It's just gathering dust.

What do you give the Dentist Of The Year?

A little plaque.

Why are leopards really bad at hide-and-seek?

They're always spotted.

My wife is complaining that I have no impulse control . . .

How would she know? We only met yesterday.

Why did the man bring his watch to the bank?

He wanted to save time.

What happened with the woman who adopted a dog from a blacksmith?

As soon as she brought it home, it made a bolt for the door.

I grilled a chicken for two hours . . .

But it still wouldn't tell me why it crossed the road.

Which felines are the best bowlers?

Alley cats.

How do you light up a sports stadium?

With a football match.

Why does a duck have feathers on its tail?

To hide its butt-quack.

Did you hear about the kidnapping at school?

The teacher woke him up.

What happens if you tell a bad chemistry joke?

You'll get no reaction.

Why did the cow go to Hollywood?

To be in the moo-vies.

The WORST -of-the- WORST JOKE!

I went to buy a pair of camouflage pants . . .

But I couldn't find any.

When is the best time to call your dentist?

Tooth-hurty.

What did the bee say to the flower?

'Hi, honey.'

What do lions have that no other animals have?

Baby lions.

What says, 'Quick! Quick!'?

A duck with hiccups.

What kind of ant can jump higher than an elephant?

Any kind – elephants can't jump.

What do you call a fake dad?

A faux pas.

What is the most popular breakfast cereal at the North Pole?

Ice Bubbles.

If pre means before and post means after . . .

Using both at the same time would be preposterous.

We argued all day about what to call a medieval soldier, but it was getting late, so . . .

We called it a knight.

What happened to the dad who started a boat-building business in his attic?

Sales went through the roof.

What do you call a cat with eight legs?

An octo-puss.

What did one potato chip say to the other?

'Let's go for a dip.'

Why shouldn't you tell jokes to a duck?

They'll quack up.

How did the piano get locked out of its car?

It lost its keys.

What do you call a rabbit with fleas?

Bugs Bunny.

How do you make an eggroll?

Push it.

I told a joke during a Zoom meeting but no-one laughed . . .
It turns out I'm not remotely funny.

I don't understand why my calculator has stopped working . . .
It just doesn't add up.

Why did the computer get glasses?

To improve its website.

Did you hear about the fire at the shoe factory?

Sadly, many soles were lost.

What do you call a cheese that isn't yours?

Nacho cheese.

Why shouldn't you trust trees?

They can be shady.

What do kids play when they have nothing else to do?

Bored games.

Did you hear about the cat that ate a lemon?

Now it's a sour puss.

When I was a kid, I was scared of the dark . . .

Now when I see my electric bill, I'm scared of the lights.

How did three elephants under one umbrella stay dry?

It wasn't raining.

Did you hear about the guy who drank invisible ink?

He's at the hospital waiting to be seen.

Is there anything worse than when it's raining cats and dogs?

Yes, hailing taxis.

What do cake and baseball have in common?

They both need a batter.

When does Friday come before Thursday?

In the dictionary.

What did the tree say when spring finally arrived?

'What a re-leaf.'

How can you tell if a pig is hot?

It's bacon.

Did you hear about the dad who was afraid of hurdles?

He got over it.

Why did the drum go to bed?

It was beat.

The WORST -of-the- WORST JOKE!

My dream job is to clean mirrors . . .

I can really see myself doing that.

What do you call a rude cow?

Beef jerky.

I saw an old man fall into a well today . . .

I guess he couldn't see that well.

What did one volcano say to the other?

'I lava you.'

Why did the computer catch a cold?

It left a window open.

How do you cook an alligator?

With a croc-pot.

What did the earthquake say when it was done?

'Sorry, my fault!'

My manager told me to have a good day . . .

So I didn't go to work.

What should you do if your puppy isn't feeling well?

Take it to the dog-tor.

What happened when the past, present and future walked into a bar?

It was tense.

Where did people hang out during medieval times?

At knight clubs.

How can you tell when a comic passes gas?

Something smells funny.

What kind of bug can tell time?

A clock-roach.

What do you call a can opener that doesn't work?

A can't opener.

What is the best way to catch a fish?

Ask someone to throw it to you.

What is a pirate's favourite letter?

The C.

Did you hear about the bossy man at the bar?

He ordered everyone around.

I've got a great joke about construction . . .
But I'm still working on it.

I only know 25 letters of the alphabet . . .
I don't know y.

What do you call a fish with no eyes?

Fsh.

Did you hear about the broken guitar for sale?

It comes with no strings attached.

Why did the roofer go to the doctor?

He had shingles.

How do you get an astronaut's baby to stop crying?

Rocket.

Why did the baseball player get arrested?

He stole third base.

What should you do if you meet a giant?

Use big words.

How do you keep a person in suspense?

I'll tell you tomorrow.

Why did the girl throw a clock out the window?

She wanted to see time fly.

Why did the baker stop making doughnuts?

He got sick of the hole business.

What is the best air to breathe if you want to be rich?

Millionaire.

Why did the king go to the dentist?

He needed to get a crown.

Why should you never trust a clock with your secrets?

Time will always tell.

Did you know that Bruce Lee had a vegan brother?

His name was Brocco Lee.

What happens when doctors get frustrated?

They lose their patients.

What do you call a bear with no teeth?

A gummy bear.

Why did the chef serve dinner late?

She ran out of thyme.

The WORST -of-the- WORST JOKE!

I received a flyer on anger management the other day . . .

I lost it.

Why did the American football coach go to the bank?

To get his quarter back.

What do you call a man wearing a rug on his head?

Matt.

Why do nurses like red crayons?

Sometimes they have to draw blood.

What kind of jewellery do rabbits wear?

14 carrot gold.

Have you ever had a bad sausage?

It's the wurst.

What did the janitor say when he jumped out of the closet?

'Supplies!'

Wisdom has been chasing me for years . . .

But I have always been faster.

Why did the girl bring a ladder on the bus?

She wanted to go to high school.

What's more unbelievable than a talking dog?

A spelling bee.

What's the best way to make a bandstand?

Take away their chairs.

What has four legs but can't walk?

A table.

Why shouldn't you play poker in the jungle?

Too many cheetahs.

What sounds like a sneeze and is made of leather?

A shoe.

How do you stop a bull from charging?

Cancel its credit card.

Why was the maths book sad?

It had too many problems.

Why are fish so smart?

They swim in schools.

I've opened three birthday cards and I'm already $150 up . . .
I love being a postman.

I don't often tell dad jokes . . .
But when I do, he laughs.

What do vampires use to catch fish?

Bloodworms.

Why was the dad fired from the keyboard factory?

He wasn't putting in enough shifts.

What do you call a girl in the middle of a tennis court?

Annette.

How is Ireland's capital city growing so quickly?

It's Dublin each year.

Did you hear about the claustrophobic astronaut?

He needed a little space.

How does an elephant hide in a strawberry patch?

It paints its toenails red.

What kind of music should you listen to while fishing?

Something catchy.

Why did the nose feel sad?

It was always getting picked on.

My wife blocked me on Facebook because I posted too many bird puns . . .

Well, toucan play that game.

My balloon elephant wouldn't fit in the back seat of my car . . .

So, I had to pop the trunk.

Where did the cat go after losing its tail?

The retail store.

How do you organise a space party?

Planet.

How do you make an octopus laugh?

Give it ten-tickles.

What do you call a potato wearing glasses?

A spec-tater.

Why did the ram run over the cliff?

It didn't see the ewe turn.

Why did the picture go to jail?

It was framed.

The WORST -of-the- WORST JOKE!

A book just fell on my head . . .

I only have my shelf to blame.

What is a calendar's favourite food?

Dates.

Why do bananas wear sunscreen?

They peel.

Why do bees have sticky hair?

They use honey combs.

Why did the watch go on holiday?

To unwind.

When is a door not a door?

When it's ajar.

How does a penguin build a house?

Igloos it together.

I told the waitress my coffee tasted like mud . . .

She replied: 'It should. It was fresh ground this morning.'

What is a sheep's favourite car?

A Lamborghini.

What kind of fish knows how to perform an appendectomy?

A sturgeon.

Did you hear about the party thrown by the walnut and the cashew?

It was nuts.

What did the roof say to the shingle?

'The first one's on the house.'

Why did the duck fall on the footpath?

It tripped on a quack.

How do birds learn to fly?

They wing it.

Why did the Oreo go to the dentist?

It lost its filling.

The policeman said he was looking for a man with one eye . . .

I told him it would be faster if he used both.

What kind of bird works on a construction site?

A crane.

My wife likes it when I blow air on her when she's hot . . .
But I'm not a fan.

I used to always be late, then I started sleeping in a herb garden . . .
Now I wake up on thyme.

Why did the phone wear glasses?

It lost all its contacts.

Did you hear about the whale that swallowed a clown?

It felt funny after.

What did the hamburger name its baby?

Patty.

How much money does a skunk have?

Just one scent.

How did the barber win the race?

He knew a shortcut.

What type of music do the planets enjoy?

Neptunes.

Lance is an uncommon name nowadays, but in medieval times . . .

People were called Lancelot.

Why did the golfer bring two pairs of pants?

Just in case he got a hole in one.

My wife asked me if I had seen the dog bowl . . .

I replied, 'I didn't know he could.'

Don't worry about your smartphone spying on you.

Your vacuum cleaner has been gathering dirt on you for years.

What is a horse's favourite TV show?

Neighbours

What do you give a scientist with bad breath?

Experi-mints.

What does an evil hen lay?

Devilled eggs.

What do you call a medieval lamp?

A knight light.

What did one hat say to the other?

'You go on ahead.'

Why did the frog take the bus to work?

His car got toad.

The WORST -of-the- WORST JOKE!

Yesterday I ate a clock . . .

It was time-consuming, especially when I went back for seconds.

What did one piece of tape say to the other?

'Let's stick together.'

What's brown and sticky?

A stick.

How does the farmer keep track of his cattle?

With a cow-culator.

What do you call a shoe made out of a banana?

A slipper.

How do you fix a broken pumpkin?

With a pumpkin patch.

Where do boats go when they're sick?

To the dock.

What did Benjamin Franklin say when he discovered electricity?

Nothing. He was too shocked.

My wife said nothing would make her happier at Christmas than receiving a diamond necklace . . .

So, I bought her nothing.

Why did the thief take a shower before robbing the bank?

He wanted to make a clean getaway.

How can you tell the difference between a dog and a tree?

By their bark.

Can February March?

No, but April May.

What do you call a fibbing cat?

A lion.

Did you hear the rumour about butter?

Well, if you haven't, I'm not going to spread it.

What's a scarecrow's favourite fruit?

Strawberries.

Where do burgers go dancing?

At the meatball.

What time do ducks wake up?

At the quack of dawn.

I used to be a banker . . .
But I lost interest.

I wanted to take a bath . . .
But I decided to leave it where it was.

What kind of tree fits in your hand?

A palm tree.

What do pigs use to clean themselves?

Hogwash.

What do you call an apology written in dots and dashes?

Re-Morse code.

Where do books hide when they're afraid?

Under their covers.

What kind of ships do vampires sail in?

Blood vessels.

What do cows like to read?

Cattle-logs.

A mummy covered in chocolate and nuts has been discovered in Egypt . . .

Archeologists believe it might be Pharaoh Roche.

What does a painter do when he gets cold?

Puts on another coat.

How can you tell the difference between a crocodile and an alligator?

One will see you later, the other will see you in a while.

Did you hear about the ice-cream truck accident?

It crashed on a rocky road.

What has four wheels and flies?

A garbage truck.

How did the farmer fix his torn overalls?

With a cabbage patch.

What do you get when you cross an elephant and a fish?

Swimming trunks.

What kind of cereal do leprechauns eat?

Lucky Charms.

What do you call recently married spiders?

Newly-webs.

What did the mother cow say to the baby cow?

'It's pasture bedtime.'

The WORST -of-the- WORST JOKE!

My kids almost caught me playing with their train set, but I threw a sheet over it just in time . . .

I think I covered my tracks.

A dragon would never explode.

But a dino might.

Why can't you trust a balloon?

It's full of hot air.

What do you call a dog in a submarine?

A subwoofer.

What do you call a bear without ears?

B.

What do you get when you cross a Smurf and a cow?

Blue cheese.

What happens when ice cream gets angry?

It has a meltdown.

Why do Norwegian navy ships have barcodes?

To Scandinavian when they come back from sea.

What do you call a locomotive carrying bubble gum?

A chew-chew train.

Why did the physics teacher break up with the biology teacher?

There was no chemistry.

A priest, a pastor and a rabbit went into a clinic to donate blood. The nurse asked the rabbit its blood type . . .

It replied: 'I'm probably a Type O.'

What invention lets you see through brick walls?

The window.

How do you know when a bike is thinking?

You can see its wheels turning.

What does a librarian use to go fishing?

A bookworm.

What did one leaf say to the other?

'I'm falling for you.'

Where's the one place you should never take your dog?

A flea market.

How does Darth Vader like his bagels?

On the dark side.

I like to sing in the car, but only when I am reversing . . .
I'm a back-up singer.

I know a joke about pizza . . .
But it's pretty cheesy.

What do you call spaghetti in disguise?

An impasta.

Where do elephants store luggage?

In their trunk.

Why do birds fly south?

Because it's too far to walk.

What do you call a fly with a sore throat?

A hoarse fly.

Where do you learn to make ice cream?

Sundae school.

Why did Wally go to therapy?

To find himself.

Why did the scarecrow become a motivational speaker?

It knew how to sow inspiration.

Someone threw a bottle of fish oil at my head . . .

I'm fine, my injuries were only super fish oil.

What do you call the pink fleshy bits between sharks' teeth?

Slow swimmers.

Why was the man banned from The Secret Cookery Society?

He kept spilling the beans.

What do you call someone who can't stick to a diet?

A desserter.

What do you call a herd of sheep falling down a hill?

A lambslide.

How do you fix a broken tomato?

With tomato paste.

What 10-letter word starts with gas?

A-U-T-O-M-O-B-I-L-E.

Why did the strawberry cry?

It got itself into a jam.

Where do astronauts go to have fun?

Lunar Park.

The WORST -of-the- WORST JOKE!

Why is e the laziest letter in the alphabet?

It's always in bed.

Why couldn't the toilet paper cross the road?

It got stuck in a crack.

What do you get from a pampered cow?

Spoiled milk.

Why can't you trust an atom?

They make up everything.

Why are pigs bad drivers?

They hog the road.

Why did police arrest the turkey?

They suspected fowl play.

What do computers eat for a snack?

Microchips.

What did the left eye say to the right eye?

'Between you and me, something smells.'

Why did the maths book become friends with the dictionary?

It wanted to improve its definition of problems.

Did you know I have an amazing ability to predict what will be inside a wrapped present?

It's a gift.

What do you call a factory that makes good products?

A satisfactory.

What do you call a group of musical whales?

An orca-stra.

What kind of birds stick together?

Velcrows.

I just flew in from Perth . . .
Boy, my arms are so tired.

Why did the tomato ask the mushroom for advice?

It was a fungi to be with.

What do you call a pile of cats?

A meowtain.

I had the perfect date last night . . .

Tomorrow, I'll have a grape.

My ceiling is great . . .
It's not the best, but it's definitely up there.

The only gift I got for Christmas was a deck of sticky playing cards . . .
I'm having a hard time dealing with it.

I haven't spoken to my wife in a week . . .

I didn't want to interrupt her.

Why did the chicken go to the seance?

To talk to the other side.

What did the hat say to the scarf?

'You hang around, and I'll go on ahead.'

Why did the computer go to bed?

It needed to crash.

Mountains aren't just funny . . .

They're hill areas.

What do a T-shirt and a banana peel have in common?

They're both easy to slip on.

What do you say to a rabbit on its birthday?

'Hoppy birthday!'

I was walking past a farm with a sign that said: Duck, eggs!

I thought the comma was unnecessary, but then it hit me.

What did the man say to his wife when he bought her the wrong type of flowers?

'Whoops, a daisy.'

Why can't Harry Potter tell the difference between his cooking pot and his best mate?

They're both cauldron.

I hate my job – all I do is crush cans all day.

It's soda pressing.

Why do fish always sing off-key?

You can't tuna fish.

Where does a sheep go to get a haircut?

The baa-baa shop.

You know what makes me smile?

My facial muscles.

What do you call a cow with no legs?

Ground beef.

Why did the banana go to the doctor?

It wasn't peeling well.

The WORST -of-the- WORST JOKE!

Every morning when I leave the house, a bike comes out of nowhere and runs me over . . .

It's a vicious cycle.

Why is blindfolded archery the best type?

You don't know what you're missing.

If you are addicted to seaweed . . .

Maybe you should sea kelp.

What time is it if you meet a crocodile?

Time to run.

What kind of streets do ghosts haunt?

Dead ends.

Did you hear about the chef who died?

She pasta way.

I'm selling some sock puppets.

Do you want to take them off my hands?

My boss said she is going to fire the employee with the worst posture . . .

I have a hunch it's going to be me.

The boy asked his dad if he had seen his sunglasses.

The dad replied, 'No. Have you seen my dadglasses?'

The waiter asked me how I found my steak.

I told him it was easy – it was right next to the potatoes.

Why should you always look in a mirror before you make a big decision?

It helps you reflect.

Orion's Belt is a big waist of space.

Terrible joke.
Only three stars.

What do you call a group of anxious dinosaurs?

Nervous Rex.

Why can't you laugh loudly in Hawaii?

They only permit a-low-ha.

Why did the runner go to the vet?

Her calves hurt.

I know you're busy, but can you say 'wonton' backwards?

'Not now.'

That's right!

Why did the coffee file a police report?

It got mugged.

It was an emotional wedding . . .
Even the cake was in tiers.

Once I read a book about glue . . .
I couldn't put it down.

What happens when frogs park illegally?

They get toad.

What has a neck but no head?

A bottle.

I wrote a book on how to not fall down stairs.

It's a step-by-step guide.

Why did the sun go to school?

To get brighter.

What do you get if you drop a piano down a mine shaft?

A flat minor.

What do Santa's elves listen to while they work?

Wrap music.

I bought my friend an elephant for his room and he said, 'Thanks.'

I replied, 'Don't mention it.'

How did the lumberjack know how many trees to cut down?

He kept a log.

Why do seagulls fly over the ocean?

Because if they flew over a bay they would be called bagels.

What weighs more: a litre of water or a litre of butane?

A litre of water. Butane is a lighter fluid.

What do you call a one-legged hippo?

A hoppo.

Why did the tailor get fired?

He wasn't a good fit.

What do you call a clown in jail?

A silicon.

Do you know what's not right?

Left.

Did you hear about the local art competition?

It ended in a draw.

Why was the belt arrested?

It held up a pair of pants.

The WORST -of-the- WORST JOKE!

My dog ate a box of Scrabble tiles, so we took him to the vet . . .

No word yet.

Why is Peter Pan always flying?

He neverlands.
(This joke never grows old.)

Last night I dreamed I was a muffler . . .

I woke up exhausted.

What did the traffic light say to the car?

'Don't look – I'm changing.'

What did the calculator say to the pencil?

'You can count on me.'

Where do rabbits go after they get married?

On a bunnymoon.

What do you call a belt made of $100 notes?

A waist of money.

What is the best thing about Switzerland?

It's hard to say, but the flag is a big plus.

As I walked home last night I passed an apple pie, a chocolate brownie and a lemon cheesecake . . .

The streets seemed strangely desserted.

What's the best way to make a fire with two sticks?

Make sure one is a match.

What did the dad say when his son spilled his peas off his dinner plate?

'Did you just pee on the floor?'

Sundays can be sad . . .

But the day before is always a sadder day.

What runs but has no legs?

A tap.

Why did the cockatoo cross the road?

To prove it wasn't a chicken.

What is black and white and black and white and black and white?

A penguin falling down stairs.

What do you call a fly with no wings?

A walk.

What happens when you wear your watch on a plane?

Time flies.

To the person who stole my runners and hi-vis jacket . . .
You can run but you can't hide.

I was going to make a joke about sodium, but . . .
Na.

What kind of tree do teeth grow on?

Gum trees.

What is an alligator's favourite shoe?

Crocs.

Why couldn't the bike stand on its own?

It was two tyred.

Did you hear the joke about the pile of paper?

It's tearable.

What kind of cage doesn't have any bars?

A rib cage.

'Dad, I feel like an ice cream.'

'That's funny, you don't look like one.'

Did you hear about the guy who invented the knock-knock joke?

He won the no-bell prize.

Why did the handyman only complete items 1, 3 and 5 on the to-do list?

He was an odd-jobs man.

What do you call someone with no body and no nose?

Nobody knows.

How did the skeleton know it was going to rain?

It could feel it in its bones.

I saw a robbery at an Apple store . . .

I guess that makes me an iWitness.

What do ministers say to get rid of insects in church?

'Let us spray.'

Wanna hear a joke about a pencil?

Actually, it's pointless.

Why are skeletons so calm?

Nothing gets under their skin.

Why did the bubble gum cross the road?

It was stuck to the chicken's foot.

What is a vampire's favourite breed of dog?

A bloodhound.

The WORST -of-the- WORST JOKE!

Nine months isn't that long . . .

But to some, it can feel like a maternity.

Why is it dangerous to start an argument in an elevator?

You can be wrong on all levels.

How can you tell when your clock is still hungry?

It goes back four seconds.

What's black and white and eats like a horse?

A zebra.

Who invented fractions?

Henry the eighth.

What is the least trustworthy metal?

Steel.

What do you call a magic dog?

A labracadabrador.

What do you call a line of men waiting to get their hair cut?

A barberqueue.

What do Bob the Builder, Alexander the Great and Oscar the Grouch have in common?

They have the same middle name.

I was up early this morning wondering what time the sun would rise . . .

Then it dawned on me.

What did the mum spaghetti say to the baby spaghetti?

'It's pasta your bedtime.'

How long is a piece of string?

Twice as long as half of it.

How do you make 7 even?

Take away the S.

Have you ever tried to catch a fog?

Yes, but I mist.

What is a florist's favourite movie?

Back to the Fuscia

What has limbs but can't walk?

A tree.

When does a joke become a dad joke?

When it becomes apparent.

I have decided that from 1 January I will only watch videos in 1080p or higher . . .
It's my New Year's Resolution.

I love telling bad puns . . .
It's just how eye roll.

Did you hear about the circus fire?

It was in tents.

What goes zzub, zzub, zzub?

A bee flying backwards.

What has five fingers but isn't your hand?

Your mum's hand.

What was the rooster doing at the gym?

Working on his pecks.

I have an inferiority complex . . .

But it's not a very good one.

What kind of dog can tell the time?

A watch dog.

What do you give a sick bird?

Emergency tweetment.

What do you call a monkey with bananas in its ears?

Anything you like – it can't hear you.

What do you get if you cross a rooster with a cocker spaniel?

A cockerdoodledoo.

A horse walks into a bar and the bartender says, 'Hey.'

The horse replies, 'Yes, thanks.'

Why did the girl give up tap dancing?

She kept falling in the sink.

Why do birds fly south for the winter?

It's too far to walk.

Why did the pony ask for a glass of water?

It was a little horse.

What does Tarzan sing at Christmas?

'Jungle Bells'

What kind of star is the most dangerous?

A shooting star.

What is striped and goes around and around?

A zebra in a revolving door.

The WORST -of-the- WORST JOKE!

Where do birds stay when they travel?

Somewhere cheep.

What do you call 26 letters going for a swim?

Alphawetical.

Why do bakers work so hard?

They knead dough.

What has five toes but isn't your foot?

My foot.

What should you do if a car runs over your toe?

Call a toe truck.

What is a dog's favourite fruit?

Pawpaw.

Dogs can't operate MRI machines . . .

But cats can.

What did the dad say as he reversed the car out of the driveway?

'Ah, this takes me back.'

Did you know that 90 percent of bald people still own a comb?

They just can't part with it.

I misplaced Dwayne Johnson's cutting tool for the origami workshop.

I can't believe I lost the Rock's Paper Scissors.

When I got fired, my company gave me a bag of used coffee . . .

They said it was grounds for termination.

When does a sandwich cook?

When it's bakin' lettuce and tomato.

What are the biggest ants in the world?

Elephants.

What do you call a group of musical frogs?

A ribbit-ing ensemble.

How do you make varnish disappear?

Take out the r.

What is green and eats porridge?

Mouldilocks.

Why was the cloud so forgetful?

It's memory was a bit cloudy.

I lost 25 percent of my roof last night . . .
oof.

I found a wooden shoe in my toilet . . .
It was clogged.

What drink is the favourite of karate kids?

Waaaa-taaaa!

Why do dragons sleep during the day?

They like to fight knights.

Did you hear about the 12-inch dog?

It was a foot long.

What do you call a puppy that sits out in the sun all day?

A hot dog.

I was mugged by six dwarves yesterday . . .

Not happy.

What kind of pie can fly?

A magpie.

If you're here for the yodelling lesson . . .

Please form an orderly, orderly, orderly queue.

If two's company and three's a crowd, what is four and five?

Nine.

Why did the man stand on one leg at the ATM?

He was checking his balance.

What do you call it when a cow grows facial hair?

A moo-stache.

How do celebrities keep cool?

They have many fans.

How do you get a mouse to smile?

Say 'cheese'.

Did you hear about the man who lost his left leg?

He's all right now.

What colour can open a car door?

Khaki.

Time flies like an arrow . . .

Fruit flies like a banana.

Why are fish so easy to weigh?

They have their own set of scales.

The WORST -of-the- WORST JOKE!

I once knew a magazine collector . . .

She had issues.

What do clouds wear beneath their pants?

Thunderwear.

What kind of bagel can travel?

A plain bagel.

What did one wall say to the other?

'I'll meet you at the corner.'

Where do penguins go to vote?

The South Poll.

What did the boy say to his fingers?

'I'm counting on you.'

How do you hire a horse?

Put up a ladder.

Why didn't the sun go to university?

It already had thousands of degrees.

The girl said she knew me from the vegetarian restaurant . . .

But I've never met herbivore.

What did one fish say to the other fish in the tank?

'Any idea how to drive this thing?'

I asked Siri why I'm so bad with women . . .

I got the reply: 'I'm Alexa, you moron.'

What do you call an anxious fly?

A jitterbug.

What do you call a happy cowboy?

A jolly rancher.

What do you call two ducks and a cow?

Quackers and milk.

What did one plate say to the other?

'Dinner's on me.'

Where do armies belong?

In sleevies.

How do mice floss their teeth?

With string cheese.

A horse walked into a bar.
The bartender said . . .
'Why the long face?'
BEST JOKE

People always told me 'icy' was an easy word to spell . . .
Now that I look at it, I see why.

How do trees get on the internet?

They log on.

What is a gazelle's favourite song?

'The Lion Sleeps Tonight'

I was arrested for drinking battery acid . . .

But I wasn't charged.

What kind of sandals do frogs wear?

Open-toad.

What did the Dalmatian say after dinner?

'That hit the spot.'

Why did the whale blush?

It saw the ocean's bottom.

What did the platypus say when it bought a lipstick?

'Put it on my bill.'

Why was the fruit bat busy on a Saturday night?

It had a date.

Why did the orange stop halfway across the road?

It ran out of juice.

What did one elevator say to the other?

'I think I'm coming down with something.'

How many apples can you grow on a tree?

All of them.

What do you call a fish wearing a bowtie?

Sophishticated.

What did the blanket say to the bed?

'I've got you covered.'

What do you call a sheep that knows karate?

A lamb chop.

Why do melons have weddings?

They cantaloupe.

Why was the traffic light late to work?

It took too long to change.

The WORST -of-the- WORST JOKE!

A cheese factory exploded in France . . .

Da brie is everywhere.

What do you call an angry fish?

Snapper.

Why did the deer go to the dentist?

It had buck teeth.

What do you call a bear in the rain?

A drizzly bear.

Why did the dad go to work in stilts?

He wanted a raise.

Why did the poodle buy a clock?

It wanted to be a watch dog.

How do you stop a pig from smelling?

Put a peg on its nose.

When I was a kid, my dad used to put me inside a tyre and roll me down a hill . . .

They were Goodyears.

What is as big as a zebra but weighs nothing at all?

A zebra's shadow.

How do you organise a fantastic space party?

You meteor expectations.

What did the lion say when it saw some kids on rollerblades?

'Meals on wheels.'

Why should you never use a dull pencil?

It's pointless.

Why aren't lobsters generous?

They're shellfish.

What do you call a cow with two legs?

Lean beef.

What causes dry skin?

A towel.

What do lawyers wear to work?

Law suits.

What did the ocean say to the beach?

Nothing. It just waved.

People are usually shocked when they find out I'm not a very good electrician.

I spent my entire life's savings on pasta . . .
It was worth every penne.

What kind of underpants do lawyers wear?

Briefs.

I started a band called Blanket . . .

It's a cover band.

What do you call a priest who becomes a lawyer?

A father-in-law.

My kids put together a PowerPoint presentation explaining why we should go to the water park . . .

It has several slides.

What did the frog say to the librarian?

'Read it, read it, read it.'

What's black and white and red all over?

A newspaper.

PENGUIN BOOKS

UK | USA | Canada | Ireland | Australia
India | New Zealand | South Africa | China

Penguin Random House Australia is part of the Penguin Random House group of companies whose addresses can be found at global.penguinrandomhouse.com.

First published by Penguin Books, an imprint of Penguin Random House Australia Pty Ltd, in 2025

Printed and bound in Australia by Griffin Press, an accredited ISO AS/NZS 14001 Environmental Management Systems printer

NATIONAL LIBRARY OF AUSTRALIA

A catalogue record for this book is available from the National Library of Australia

FSC
www.fsc.org
MIX
Paper | Supporting responsible forestry
FSC® C018684

ISBN 978 1 76 135447 2 (Paperback)

We at Penguin Random House Australia acknowledge that Aboriginal and Torres Strait Islander peoples are the Traditional Custodians and the first storytellers of the lands on which we live and work. We honour Aboriginal and Torres Strait Islander peoples' continuous connection to Country, waters, skies and communities. We celebrate Aboriginal and Torres Strait Islander stories, traditions and living cultures; and we pay our respects to Elders past and present.